TOO MUCH KISSING!

To Natalie and Sol,
two wonderful parents
who taught me how
—A. K.

To Deborah
—D. C.

MARGARET K. MCELDERRY BOOKS
An imprint of Simon & Schuster Children's Publishing Division
1230 Avenue of the Americas, New York, New York 10020
Text copyright © 2010 by Alan Katz
Illustrations copyright © 2010 by David Catrow
For information about special discounts for bulk purchases, please contact Simon & Schuster
Special Sales at 1-866-506-1949 or business@simonandschuster.com.
The Simon & Schuster Speakers Bureau can bring authors to your live event.
For more information or to book an event, contact the Simon & Schuster Speakers Bureau
at 1-866-248-3049 or visit our website at www.simonspeakers.com.
Book design by Sonia Chaghatzbanian
The text for this book is set in Kosmik.
The illustrations for this book are rendered in watercolors, colored pencil, and ink.
Manufactured in China
2 4 6 8 10 9 7 5 3
Library of Congress Cataloging-in-Publication Data
Katz, Alan.
Too much kissing!: and other silly dilly songs about parents / Alan Katz ; illustrated by David Catrow.
— 1st ed.
p. cm.
Summary: Set to the tunes of well-known songs, provides new, humorous lyrics about
mothers and fathers.
ISBN 978-1-4169-4199-6
1. Children's songs, English—United States—Texts. 2. Parents—Songs and music—Texts.
[1. Parents—Songs and music. 2. Songs.] I. Catrow, David, ill. II. Title.
PZ8.3.K1275To 2009
782.42—dc22
[E]
2008023001

TOO MUCH KISSING!

AND OTHER SILLY DILLY SONGS ABOUT PARENTS

WRITTEN BY **ALAN KATZ**

ILLUSTRATED BY **DAVID CATROW**

MARGARET K. McELDERRY BOOKS
NEW YORK LONDON TORONTO SYDNEY

They're Always on the Cell
(To the tune of "Farmer in the Dell")

My mommy's on her cell.
My daddy's on his cell.
They don't talk to each other, but
they're always on the cell.

Dad's talking by the hour.
Right now he's in the shower.
He made a call right in the stall
(it's hooked to a cell tower).

A gadget on Mom's ear
is there so she can hear.
It's nuts, here's proof: She's on the roof.
That's where the signal's clear.

I just sit here and sigh,
but yet I never cry.
On Tuesday nights they both take time
to call me and say hi.

I Am on a Schedule
(To the tune of "Twinkle, Twinkle, Little Star")

I am on a schedule,
that is why my day is full.
Three p.m. is chess,
then math;
5:07, take a bath;
dry off, then laps in the pool.
So much learning after school!

Next day starts with martial arts,
tuba lessons, then it's darts,
soccer practice, photo club,
off to Scouts—I'm still a Cub—
Spanish (teacher's from Madrid):
Don't they know I'm just a kid?

Golf and tennis, flute and harp,
fishing (Hey, I caught a carp!),
boxing, bowling, yoga, clay.
Wish I could go out and play.
Mom has got my whole week planned.
I'm stretched like a rubber band!

Weekend comes, and that's the best:
It's when Mommy lets me rest.
I can kick back and relax,
'cept for magic, cooking, sax,
science, gardening, and tap.
Next May 3rd I get to nap!

Disgusting Things
(To the tune of "My Favorite Things")

Entrees so yucky and
side dishes squishy,
meals that for days make the house smell all fishy.
Can't bear to see what tonight's dinner brings.
Mom and Dad eat only disgusting things.

Everything's sticky, spicy, and revolting.
Filleted, sautéed, I don't care—it's still molting.
I'd rather munch on our wood napkin rings
than take a bite of their disgusting things.

Sauces heaping,
Mom's food's creeping—
it just ate her peas.
My parents cook food that I can't stand, so I'll
have three meals a day . . . grilled cheese!

Dad's Driving Me Crazy
(To the tune of "Sidewalks of New York")

Left lane,
right lane,
all around the road.
My daddy just passed a Honda
at such speed we might explode.
He zipped off the highway,
down the ramp we bulldozed.
Hope his eyes are open,
because mine are tightly closed!

Fast lane,
slow lane,
zooming in and out.
Breaking the sound barrier—
can't hear other drivers shout.
Dad shows off his turbo,
his five-speed, and his torque.
He should not be driving
on the sidewalks of New York!

My Mother Just Rushes
Through Bedtime

(To the tune of "My Bonnie Lies Over the Ocean")

My mother just rushes through bedtime.
With stories, she sure cuts them short.
If she keeps this up, you can bet I'm
Taking her to fairy tale court.

Mother, Mother,
I know that down deep you do care, do care.
But, oh brother,
Goldilocks met more than one bear!

My mother just zips right through bedtime.
With books, she turns pages by twos.
While she races out to watch prime time,
I lie in the dark so confused.

Mother, Mother,
through another story you've blown, you've blown.
And, oh brother,
Jill didn't fetch water alone!

My mother just blitzes through bedtime.
I don't mean to moan or nitpick.
I listened, but here in my head I'm
sure it's not *Jack and the Beanstick*!

Mother, Mother,
please sometime a whole story tell, do tell.
Mother, Mother.
Love, your only child . . . Hansel!

Watch Dad Exercise
(To the tune of "Do Your Ears Hang Low?")

Watch Dad exercise!
See him work his upper thighs
as he runs and lifts and bends—
how he grunts and squints his eyes!
The whole room is kinda sweaty.
Is he done? Oh no, not yet;
he does more exercise!

Watch Dad exercise!
Time for weights, and so he tries
to pick up our baby grand,
which he does, to my surprise.
"Put it down," my sis keeps saying.
(At the moment, she is playing!)
Dad loves exercise!

Watch Dad exercise!
When he's finished, he drip-dries.
Mom then says, "Let's paint the den."
(Something Daddy does despise.)
So he says, "That workout's sapping.
If you need me, I'll be napping!"
Too much exercise!

Dressed Up Is Messed Up

(To the tune of "The Battle Hymn of the Republic")

My mom says there's a party, and I know just what that means:
I'm gonna have to change out of these soiled, hole-filled jeans.
No question it will lead to one of those annoying scenes.
I hate to wear nice clothes!

I can't stand all the fancy-schmantzy antsy-causing shirts,
but my sister is so thrilled; she'll choose from forty-seven skirts.
I got two shiny shoes; the left one's scuffed, the right one hurts.
I hate to wear nice clothes!

When it's time to get all dressed up,
to me, that is oh so messed up.
And to Mom and Dad I 'fessed up:
I hate to wear nice clothes!

When we got to the party, everybody stopped to stare.
And guess who was the only boy dressed up in formal wear?
Did Mommy learn her lesson? I don't know, and I don't care.
Next time I'm staying home!

Too Much Kissing!
(To the tune of "Rock-a-bye Baby")

Each morning, when my folks
head to work,
they do something
that drives me berserk:
She puckers up
and then so does he,
and that's when my parents
get all kissy!

Late afternoon, they're back
in the house.
Dad says to Mom,
"How's my loving spouse?"
She gives a hug,
and then, woe is me,
I have to watch them
get all kissy!

When I get married—
just wait and see—
I will refuse to
get all kissy!
Kisses are only
good, in my mind,
when foil-wrapped, like
the chocolate kind!

They're Full of Beans
(To the tune of "Take Me Out to the Ball Game")

Mom and Dad just drink coffee.
They both live on caffeine.
Each has a pot before starting work,
while at their jobs they are on auto-perk,
and it's brew, brew, brew after dinner.
It's like a java monsoon!
It's no wonder they haven't slept
a wink since last June!

Mom and Dad just drink coffee—
extra strong, no decaf.
Every week they each brew twenty pounds.
Coffee pot broke, so they just ate the grounds.
And if they don't stop drinking coffee,
I fear that someday they will
want to pack up all of our stuff
and move to Brazil!

Seeing Is Believing
(To the tune of "Itsy Bitsy Spider")

Mom said she lost her glasses
while working in the yard.
That was a break for me—
I'd come home with my report card.
I said I'd read it to her.
You see, this was my hunch:
She wouldn't see the C I got
in everything but lunch.

My plan was really brilliant;
at least it seemed to me.
I stood and boasted, "My grades are
A, A, A, A, A, B!"
Then Mom got real excited—
can't get her to relax.
I'm in my room and punished:
Who knew she wore contacts?

Petting Is Getting Upsetting
(To the tune of "Happy Birthday")

I would sure like a pet,
but my folks say not yet
'cause they're hairy and smelly,
and they're frequently wet.

I asked Dad for a bird,
but he just squawked, "Absurd!"
When I begged for a kitten,
"No way," my mother purred.

I would so love a dog
or a hamster or frog.
They would surely be cleaner
than my brother, the hog.

With the pleading, I'm through;
so no duck, snake, or gnu.
I am petless, there's nothing
to cock-a-doodle-doo!

Mind Your Reminders
(To the tune of "This Old Man")

Mom reminds
me each day,
"Comb your hair!"
"Put toys away!"
"Do your homework!"
"Read a book!"
"Turn off that TV!"
What does Mommy want from me?

Dad reminds
me each day,
"Brush your teeth,
fight tooth decay!"
"Take your vitamins!"
"Practice for the
spelling bee!"
What does Daddy want from me?

I don't know
how they find
all the time just
to remind,
but they've got a list
when I wake up each a.m.
Wonder who's reminding them?

The Allowance Song
(To the tune of "Home on the Range")

It's allowance day,
so "Good morning," I say
as my mom hands my
weekly amount.
Later, Dad has to dash,
so he gives me some cash,
and says, "Here's your allowance, please count!"

Yes, I collect twice,
which perhaps you might think
isn't nice.
They're so busy,
I doubt
that they'll ever
find out.
(Send me ten bucks for this great advice!)

Folks' Conversation
(To the tune of "Down by the Station")

Folks' conversation—
don't know what they're saying.
One is "in a pickle,"
other "spilled the beans";
she is "in a jam" now,
he's "walking on eggshells."
Do they work inside our fridge?
That's what I think it means.

Folks' conversation—
totally confusing.
He says, "Work's a madhouse,"
she has to "pitch in";
he's "behind the eight ball,"
she's "over a barrel."
I would like to help them,
but where do I begin?

Folks' conversation . . .
I decide to join them.
I say, "School's a sandwich."
"Playground ate the hen."
"Homework has me shoe store."
"My room makes me tonsil."
Mom and Dad go back to
speaking real again!